Dzvinka Torokhtushko

THE LADYBUG

Artist Alexander Kurylo

A fairy tale for children and more...

Amazon.com

This is another story of goodness and light. This is a story that teaches not to be afraid, but to overcome even those obstacles that seem insurmountable.

Don't be afraid to be small. If you want, you can do everything. For it is not the strong who are great and strong physically, but the one who has great strength of spirit and a good heart.

© Dzvinka Torokhtushko, 2020
© Illustrated by Alexandr Kurylo, 2020

ISBN: 9798427419086
Imprint: Independently published

It happens! You are tiny and weak in the big and troubled world. The world, where the novitiates and dangers are waiting for you. It wants sometimes to give up in despair.

But... you cannot. Because you are a little bit the Ladybug!

And you still know that your Angel is nearby you. Nobody sees him, but you know – he is. And just at the moment when your hands fall, your Angel will hover over you with his wings.

Because it happens...

The lady-bug's name was Zlatko and he was not a Lady, but a little beetle-boy, so his Grandpa called him just Buggy. The Grandpa was big, strong and brave; he had long whis-kers and wings with so many spots that Buggy even wasn't able to count them. After all, what's the difference how many spots dotted Grandpa's wings? The main thing is that Buggy's Grandpa loved him. That's what Buggy thought.

Buggy was very little, almost tiny. Only three spots dotted his thin almost transparent wings. Yes, you are right – Buggy was only three insect years old. He lived in a hut, built in a crack of old linden bark.

Well, it`s people usually see there only a deep crack, but in fact, there's a small hut that was built by Buggy's Grandpa – the old and wise Luga. He was really wise bug. He knew a lot of things. All fairy tales in the world were known to him. He was the Master-of-Time. No matter how long the winter evenings were, but they flew almost in the blink of an eye with the Grandpa's tales! One fairy tale went after another until sweet dreams came to you. And dreams were colourful and fabulous, too.

Buggy was sure that Grandpa whiskered colours into his dreams. Only by the time Buggy was still asking:

– Grandpa, how is it so? Well, your whiskers are white, but the dreams are colourful and bright!

The Grandpa smiled:

– Do you remember the summer flowers, the minty coolness and green blooms? That's always so, Buggy. The colours of the summer flowers turn into winter dreams. And do you remember the linden tree blossoms? You see, it is because of linden trees blossom dreams become sweet. Sweet like linden tree honey is.

Moreover, the Grandpa knew the names of all the flowers in the world. He could sense what the trees were whispering about in the wind and what the grass kept silent about, he knew where all the white clouds were floating. And also he knew from where the forest stream started, the one which ran behind the dog-roses bushes. And he believed that the river ended somewhere far from the forest, turned into a blue and deep sea. The sea, where big and hefty fish lived. The sea fish were much larger than the bleak, the roach, the trout and even the old mirror carp living in the Alder Pond near the Dark Whirlpool.

Buggy was kidding gently at the Grandpa's tales and beliefs. But really, how possibly can a small forest stream, getting so narrow and shallow during the summer heat, turn into a large and deep sea?

"That's all nothing but fairy tales for grown-ups," Buggy believed. "Everything in the world should be comparable. If there are fairy tales for kids, full of small miracles and wonders, then there should also be fairy tales for grown-ups. And the miracles in those tales must be so great that adults would believe in them. Otherwise what kind of an adult could ever believe in a small miracle?"

Of course, Buggy had his Dad and Mom, Brothers and Sisters, but he lived with his Grandfather. Brothers and Sisters were big enough and went to school in the city, and his Father and Mother worked a lot.

Buggy was a little boy and got sick too often. Therefore, his wings were not red, but so clear, almost transparent not like those of the other lady-bugs and the spots on his wings were barely visible. As soon as the nasty weather broke out in the forest, Buggy got high temperature, his eyes filled up with tears and he got a barking cough.

Grandpa Luga used all his knowledge of medicinal herbs, took Buggy to famous doctors and healers and also to the Salt Lake. They even visited Professor Dragon Fly, the famous entomologist. Sadly, nobody

knew what to do and how to help. Every time the rainy weather sets, Buggy starts coughing.

Because of the illness, he could not fly as his peers. That is why he was sitting in the sun and watching the other guys-bugs playing on the forest lawn. He was watching them, catching warm rays and poplar fluff, flying from one flower to another, and he was sighing sadly.

Grandpa Luga also was sighing sadly and anxiously. And every morning he read carefully the lines of a forest newspaper, he looked for a message about well-known and unknown doctors who came to the forest dwellers from the foreign lands.

He always listened carefully to the reports of the forest radio, broadcasted by the well-informed journalist Mrs Piet Chatterbox. Though the whole forest considered Mrs Piet Chatterbox to be a gossiper and a liar, the Grandpa listened to her attentively, what she was smearing about from an old stork nest, placed on an abandoned electric pillar. He never lost the hope to cure Buggy.

One day the Grandpa read that the famous Master-of-Forest-Medicine from a faraway Ita-lian land, Dr Miele d`Api Bee would hand around his miraculous medicines from all known and unknown diseases on the Shadowy Meadow at the northern edge of the forest, just beyond the hill.

Of course, there is no medicine like hope, and old Grandpa Luga hurried to the Shadowy Meadow. And Buggy was left waiting at home.

Well, not really at home. How could someone stay at home when it is summer in full swing, the sun is shining brightly and flowers flourish everywhere?! The playful colourful butterflies are floa-ting all over above the flowers as if inviting him to fly with them.

"I wish I were a butterfly when I am grown up", Buggy was day-dreaming. Then he quietly rushed down a rustling bark, settled by the

old linden under a strawberry bush, and started admiring the bright colours of the day.

He wasn't sad or bored, no way! The strawberry bush grew just on the edge of an ant path, and hard-nosed ants were running back and forth, carrying woodchips, stalks, and leaves on their shoulders. Sometimes they stopped for rest and for a small chat with Buggy, and afterwards went back to their ant business again.

Buggy was admiring the high sky and the tall trees holding it. Well, that's how it seemed to him. The trees were so high above and overhead that they could scatter the clouds floating over and shading the warm sun from time to time.

Everything around smelled of thyme, mint, ripe berries and something so dear and tender that Buggy was almost dizzy.

"It must be the chamomile or marjoram", he mused.

He remembered the flavour of a marjoram potion that his Grandpa used to brew to warm up his little feet when Buggy caught a cold near a frozen window in winter. And he could almost smell tart chamomile tea steaming from a small mug.

"Some ill-timed memories," Buggy thought. – While summer is raging, the sun is shining and flowers are flourishing I suddenly recalled winter teas..."

All of a sudden a strong blast of wind blew off the peaceful tranquillity of the day. The wind brought large and grey clouds hung them all over the woods and roared with laughter. Somewhere high in the sky a lightning strike flashed and then another one. And then a thunderbolt roared. The furious gusts of the wind were tearing out the leaves from the trees, trampling grass and flowers into the ground, and then again shooting up high in the sky as if to shake off heavy rain from the gloomy clouds.

The ants were hurrying and streaming to their anthill. Beetles, butterflies and all the fo-rest tiny creatures were rushing to their homes. The Buggy was so frightened that he could hardly move. He was trembling with all his claws and flaps under a strawberry leaf and was scared to move around.

The wind wasn't calming down it was twisting and raging all over the meadow. It was completely dark, the lightings were striking like fire arches over the forest, the thunder did not quench. The first large heavy drops of rain were already falling from the nasty leaden clouds.

Buggy decided to flee as fast as possible to the hut. But as soon as he put his leg above the root of the old linden he heard someone's crying. There was a little Ant sitting on the path.

"What's happened?" Buggy asked.

"I must have twisted my leg… The knee is damaged … It hurts so much! I cannot go" the Ant was sobbing. "Help me, please!"

The Buggy was hesitating. At first, he thought that the anthill was so far away, and then that his Grandpa would scold him. Like when it happened when Buggy was careless and overturned Grandpa's pots with morning dew. But he didn't mean it, it was really so incautious of him. The Buggy was wondering what was inside those jars and pots.

The rain was becoming heavier and heavier, more and more drops were falling down. And soon the ant path began to look like a stormy stream among the high summer greenery. And the stream was about to pick up the little Ant with its waves and carry to the middle of nowhere.

"Hold on for me!" Buggy ran up to the Ant and bent down low enough so that she could get up to his back. She did not have to be asked twice.

However, a sharp blast of wind drove Ant down.

"Oh! What to hold on to? It is so slippery on your wings…"

"You should climb up and hold on to my shoulders. I have shoulders under my wings. You wouldn't slip away at them. You would be safe there."

The Ant gripped firmly onto Buggy's shoulders, and they were off through the stormy weather, through the rain and the wind to the anthill.

The storm was raging all over the forest. It was getting dark as if suddenly a late night was outside. There was not a single firefly gleaming above the path where they used to live; all of them were burrowing in the holes. And the path itself could hardly be seen in a few short glimpses when another lightning was flashing.

It was a long way to go, it was slippery and spooky. Nobody knows who could be hiding behind that nettle bush or that branch lying fell in the middle of the path.

The Buggy was scared and the little Ant seemed to be heavier and heavier with every step. As if she was absorbing rainwater like a sponge plant the Grandfather once told him about.

Suddenly, there was a new crimp on a hard and endless path. Right in front of Buggy a huge hill of grass, leaves and last year's fir needles began to grow from below the ground. The hump was growing very quickly. It was budging and buzzing loudly from time to time.

The Buggy was frightened and stopped.

"What's there?" the Ant asked in a whisper.

"I don't know," murmured Buggy. "It's something big and scary."

"I am not something!" The hump was shouting. "I am someone! I am a Beetle! Yes! The Beetle!"

The Beetle finally got to the surface. He was big, strong, with black eyes and twisted horns. The Beetle had brilliant brown-red wings and strong legs.

"Uncle Beetle!" Buggy said enthusiastically. "How nice you are here!"

"Of course it's nice!" Beetle agreed. "It's always nice where I am."

"Uncle Beetle!" The Buggy was still glowing with joy, "Little Ant hurt her knee. Would you help her to get home?"

"Whaaat-oh?" The beetle was so surprised that crouched on both pairs of his back legs.

"I hurt and scratched my leg," the Ant started to whimper.

"Terrribbble!" the Beetle replied.

"Help us, please, Uncle Beetle! Buggy is as small as me. But he is also sick; he is coughing and is completely dropping. And there's a thunderstorm soaring and it's raining heavily... And you're so big and strong, you have to make just a few steps to the anthill!"

"Terrribbble!" the Beetle bawled again. "Do you really suggest that I, such a great and grand Beetle in this forest, should go down so that all sorts of careless little things could be picked up on the trail?

Moreover, they have to be carried somewhere?! Alas, the times, and the manners! Terrribbble! The children are no longer taught decency nowadays."

"But we asked politely!" The Buggy was surprised.

"We said "please" the Ant supported him.

"So what? Does it make any difference? Such small and minor bugs like you should have stepped aside from my path before I saw you! You should stand still and bow down until I pass you by. Help them, huh! Terribbble!"

"But isn't it noble to help others, those who are smaller and weaker?" The Buggy was curious.

"Terrribbble!" the Beetle shouted again. "Who told you that? It's such a nonsensical nonsense, such an illogical, unwise opinion, such an empty phrase!"

"It was my Grandpa…" Buggy stared at the Beetle standing opposite with his open wings, with horns raised high and his sparkling fierce eyes.

"Terrribbble! Your Grandfather is an old unwise minor bug."

"My Grandpa is a lady-bug! He is the best Grandpa in the whole world! He is wise and knows a lot of fairy tales."

"And he feeds you up with tales!" the Beetle said. "Nobleness is beauty, strength, and greatness! Nobleness is in wings, horns, and claws. This is a breed. And it's a privilege for big beetles, but not for such minor guys as you and your Grandfather."

"My Grandpa is kind!" Buggy objected.

"But only the strongest survive!" the Beetle answered.

And he went on the path back to his own great and grand business. And what else kind of business such great and grand Beetle could have? Deeply inside Buggy thought that the Beetle surely was grand and strong, but too nosewise because of his own grandeur.

"What a slicker!" that was Buggy's exact mind, and then he sighed deeply and coughed rough.

The Buggy was coughing for a long time. And long after that cough he was catching his breath. He saw pink circles in front of his eyes, he was dizzy and his wings hurt.

The path was wet from the rain and there were drowned leaves of grass on it. It seemed to be endless for him. The anthill was still not visible on a close horizon and Buggy was helpless and weak.

However, he managed to get up on his legs and moved forward. He made his way through the wet grass under the wet foliage of plantain and the coltsfoot between the weighed small marigolds and dandelions that buried their yellow curly heads in the leaves.

The ant was sitting on his back, tightly clutching his shoulders with her claws and trembling.

"What's wrong?" Buggy asked.

"It's cold," replied the Ant. "It's a long way to go. Nasty weather is raging. If you had left me, you would have been warmed up in your hut. But look what's now…"

"Well …" Buggy smiled. "Sorry that I'm not so grand and noble to leave you."

"Thank you!" the little Ant whispered. "You are the noblest one in the world!"

"Grandpa has probably been worried already…" Buggy thought and stopped.

The creepy wind was blowing so fiercely that Buggy could hardly stand and he fell down. The little Ant slid between his wings and slipped on a wet path. She must have hurt herself, because she sobbed a few

times, burst into tears and cried out loudly like little girls would cry when they hurt the knee.

"Ah-ah! We are sure to get lost! I'm scared!" the Ant cried.

"Don't be scared, everything will be fine," Buggy tried to calm her down. "I'm sure to have carried you."

He was reassuring her so confidently as if he was used to carrying little ants with hurting knees every day.

Actually, Buggy was breathing hard, and the bad cough had already come back with a heavy wheezing. The legs were painful, the wings fell down and he was terribly sleepy. He wished he could sleep right here amidst the thunderstorm on the wet path...

"Oh nooo! You won't have carried me!" the Ant kept weeping.

"Sure I will!" Buggy hushed at her. "I'm a boy! I'm brave and strong!"

And they hit the road again. They went through the thunderstorm and the darkness, overcoming the grass clinging down close to the path and they were bypassing the broken twigs and the fallen leaves. Buggy often stopped, sometimes he was coughing for a long time, but then he was going on. On their way, he even managed to tell little Ant tales he had heard from his Grandpa.

However, the Ant seemed to be heavier with every step and their way seemed to be longer and longer. The storm was still-timed and terribly long-lasting. The grass was like wildered web, all slippery and wet from the rain. The darkness was murky and muddy like in a blackened fog.

Even when it was pretty close to the anthill it still seemed to Buggy that he had quite a long way to go. He was short of breath, his cough was getting worse and almost stifling, everything was dizzy and stirring up in a muddy mist.

When all the ant family ran out from their anthill to meet them with flashing fireflies all of a sudden Buggy got so scared that he fell down on the cold path and fainted.

The next morning the sun was shining brightly through the windows of the anthill. All the trees, the grass and flowers were so bright and eye-catching. No wonder that the rain-washed forest always seems more colourful and bright.

Buggy stretched and yawned on a warm-fluffy dandelion cot.

"Oh look! Our hero has woken up!" Someone whispered nearby.

Buggy turned his head and saw a worried Grandpa. It seemed that his whiskers were even more whitewashed and he became somewhat smaller or something.

"I'm so sorry, Grandpa!" Buggy jumped from the cot, but suddenly he was frightened by his tinkling voice.

Grandpa looked at him with astonishment. Then he grabbed him by the wing and pulled out of the anthill.

Buggy shuddered. His Grandfather used to do everything slowly and calmly and now there was such rushing hurry...

"Repeat it again!" the Grandfather ordered outside.

Tears rushed into Buggy's eyes and yesterday's rain was nothing compared to them.

All the dwellers of the anthill gathered nearby. There was the little Ant with a bandaged knee. There was someone big and shaggy, in a white hat with a flower and in a striped suit that looked out from under a white robe.

"It must be Dr Miele d`Api bee!" Buggy made a guess.

"Oh! I told you that my mixsturino with chlorophyll, propolis and mushroom elixir is miraculous!" The doctor was buzzing. "Look! Bambino is absolutely healthy and fit. Gracie ovatio!"

"Yeah!" The Old Ant chuckled and winked. "It's good only to water the lungwort or moss on the stump."

"No way!" Dr Miele d`Api bee was indignant. "My mixsturino has a healing effect. It has a perfect healing effect on broken horns. Look at this great hero, whom we will make grandiose grace today!"

Buggy turned his head to the side the doctor pointed.

The Beetle was sitting near the anthill under the leaf of a burdock. The very same Beetle they saw walking proudly through the rain yesterday. A strong and large Beetle now had a bandaged horn, a swollen eye and an unfair look. His red-brown wings were scratched from the sides as if they were stripping off the colour. And his big bald feet were all muddy and dirty.

The ants were fussing around him. Some of them were carrying water in the blue-bells' jars, others were dipping grass sponges into the water and wiping Beetle's wings.

"Oh! How diffficult it isss to walk againssst the wind!" the Beetle said.

"Oh-oh-horrror! And it's even more difficult to s-s-struggle with the wind. It is under the power of only the courrrageous and nobbble beetles!"

And he was shaking his head and wings. The small ants sighed in a chorus, staring at the Beetle with great enthusiasm and continued their work.

"Noble! Ah-ha! Noble beetle!" The Buggy was outraged.

"What's up?" the Old Ant asked. "We barely brought him here. We found him on the Chimeric Lawn lying half-dead. We were all dried out and exhausted as we pulled him out of the shrubs of dope and henbanes."

"What was he doing on the Chimeric Lawn?" Grandpa Luga was interested.

"He was struggling with the wind. He said he had been stopping yesterday's storm."

"Wow! He must be really noble. Dope and henbanes are very helpful against the wind. And belladonna is blooming now on the Chimeric Lawn!" Buggy remarked.

"Oh, Bambino!" Dr Miele d`Api Bee exclaimed. "Belladonna is a poisonous plant. It makes head dizzy and eyes foggy. Belladonna is not belle, it's a dope!"

"That's right!" Buggy agreed.

"What was not right?" The Old Ant gazed at Buggy.

And then Buggy told how a noble Beetle had refused to help them yesterday.

"What a wicked and mean beetle!" The ants exclaimed altogether.

"Fecalio!" Dr Miele d`Api Bee shouted.

"What a dor-bug! What a scoundrel!" Grandpa Luga was outraged.

"What a rascal!" The Old Ant summed up.

All the ants rolled out in a wave from the Beetle. He could hardly stand up.

"Well, okay, okay! Well, I lied to you! So what? Let bygones be bygones. And now I'm wounded and I need help.

"Oh!" Dr Miele d`Api Bee smirked. "I know a very effective remedy just for such case. It's the best of my mixtures. Panacea!"

"Let's try it!" The Beetle was eager.

"Oh yeah! But I would ask Senor Beetle to apologize first."

"No way! No apologies for the minors! Oh, horrribbble! It will never happen! Treat me quickly! What's your got, doctor?"

"I have some special treatment just for your condition, Senor Beetle. It's called api-therapy."

"What is this?" the Beetle wondered. "After all, what's the difference? The main point is that my horns should be beautiful."

"It's a bumble bee sting. It has a miraculous healing effect on horns and good manners..."

All the ants burst into laughter and Dr Miele d`Api Bee buzzed loudly, straightened his wings, spinning them so fast that the air was swirling. Then he tweaked the sting and flew up into the air.

The Beetle stared at him without the slightest understanding and then shouted:

– Terrribbble! Help! Help!

And he rushed as fast as he could into the thicket of the high grass behind the anthill.

"Oh! What a terribly scared hero!" Dr Miele d`Api Bee chuckled.

"Come on! Some hero!" Grandfather Luga shouted. "He is a very ordinary dor-beetle."

"Exactly!" the Old Ant concluded. "Imagine him struggling with the wind! Every ass loves to hear itself bray!"

The ants burst out laughing again and started whispering with each other. Then they lined up in a semicircle and shouted all together:

"Thank you, Buggy!"

Buggy got terribly embarrassed. He used to be a small, pale, ever coughing lady-bug, who didn't do anything extraordinary, and now so many ants were grateful. Buggy wanted to hide away, at least behind his Grandpa. But his Grandfather stepped aside and looked at him closely.

"He must have been really worried!" The Buggy was thinking.

He was so sorry that he made his Grandfather anxious. But he couldn't possibly leave the little Ant all by herself...

Buggy shifted from foot to foot and looked away.

"Well, how are you, Buggy?" the Old Ant asked. "I see you are better now. You frightened all of us. You're seemed to be such a brave knight but fainted at the sight of a shimmering firefly. Unbelievable!"

Buggy got even more ashamed.

"You are our hero!" the Old Ant said.

"Oh, yes, Bambino! You are a real hero!"

"All well that ends well!" Grandpa Luga summed up and patted Buggy on the cheek. "Now, tell us something!"

Buggy could not say a word for a long time as if he was choked with embarrassment and awkwardness.

"I'm so sorry, Grandpa!" He whispered at last.

"Come on!" Grandpa waved his claws. "Well done! I am so proud of you."

"Oh! You are so kind!" the little Ant came up to Buggy. "But for you, I would have died. You have really strong shoulders and strong wings."

The little Ant hugged him with his thin claws. Buggy got terribly embarrassed and then he got red!

THE END!

Dzvinka Torokhtushko

THE LADYBUG

Artist Alexander Kurylo

ISBN: 9798427419086
Imprint: Independently published